Quiz: 6212921

Leve

P9-BZX-696

Points: 0.5

Watch, the Superdog!

CREATED BY

Gertrude Chandler Warner

ILLUSTRATED BY

Kay Life

Albert Whitman & Company

Morton Grove, Illinois

You will also want to read:
Meet the Boxcar Children
A Present for Grandfather
Benny's New Friend
The Magic Show Mystery
Benny Goes into Business
Watch Runs Away
The Secret under the Tree
Benny's Saturday Surprise
Sam Makes Trouble

Library of Congress Cataloging-in-Publication Data
Warner, Gertrude Chandler, 1890-1979
Watch, the superdog! / created by Gertrude Chandler Warner;
illustrated by Kay Life.
p. cm. — (The Adventures of Benny & Watch; #10)
Summary: Benny decides to enter his dog Watch in the local pet parade,
but Watch ruins his costume while saving a nest of baby birds from a cat.
ISBN 0-8075-0647-8
[1. Dogs—Fiction. 2. Pets—Fiction. 3. Parades—Fiction.]
I. Life, Kay, ill. II. Title.
PZ7.W244 Wav 2002
[E]—dc21
2002003467

Henry

Violet

Jessie

Grandfather

Watch

Benny

The Boxcar Children

Henry, Jessie, Violet, and Benny Alden are orphans. They are supposed to live with their grandfather, but they have heard that he is mean.

So the children run away and live in an old red boxcar. They find a dog, and Benny names him Watch.

When Grandfather finds them, the children see that he is not mean at all. They happily go to live with him. And, as a surprise, Grandfather brings the boxcar along!

Grandfather, Benny, and Watch were at the pet store. Watch needed dog food and biscuits.

Benny saw a sign. It said, "Pet Parade Saturday."

On the window signs:

Lou's
PET
Shop

Children's
Pet Parade
All pets welcome!
NEXT
Saturday
11am–1pm
register at City Hall

Grandfather read, "All pets welcome. Win a prize!"

Benny was excited. He had never been in a parade before. Maybe Watch could win!

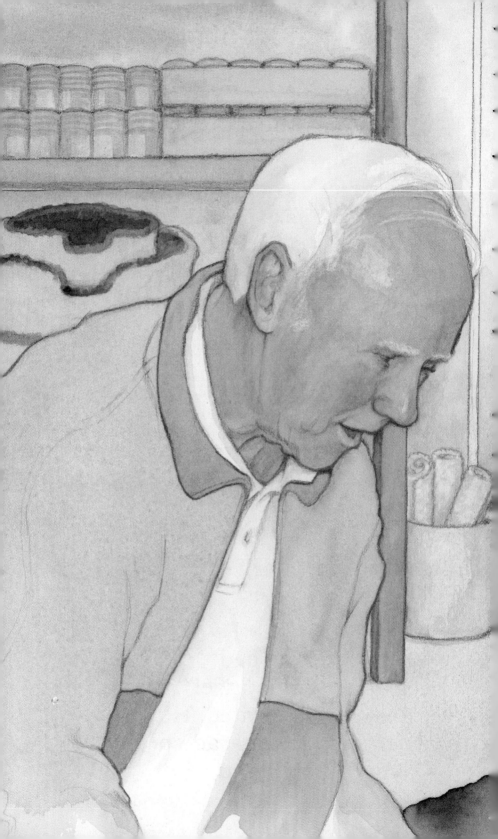

"Grandfather, can Watch and I be in the parade?" asked Benny.

"Sure!" said Grandfather. "The poster says you need to sign up at City Hall."

"Let's go tomorrow," said Benny.

"Woof!" said Watch.

The next day, Benny, Watch,
and Grandfather went to City Hall.
Grandfather helped Benny fill
out the entry form. "Prizes are
given to the biggest and smallest
pets," read Grandfather. "Also for
pets wearing good costumes."

"Watch is not very big, and he's not very small. But I want him to win a prize," said Benny. "So I'll have to think of a great costume."

That night Benny thought very
hard. "How about a clown? Or a
cowboy? Or a monster?" he asked
Watch.

Watch was sniffing under
Benny's bed. He found some
cookie crumbs there.

"You're always looking for stuff,"
said Benny. "That gives me an
idea. You can be a detective!"

The next day, Jessie helped
Benny make a coat for Watch.

Benny found an old hat. He put it on Watch's head. "Perfect!" Benny said. "You look just like a dog detective."

On Saturday, Benny woke up early. "Come on, let's go outside, Watch," he called. "I'll give you a bath. You need to look good for the parade."

But Watch didn't want a bath. Instead, he ran over to a tree. He sniffed around it.

"Watch," said Benny. "What are you doing?"

Benny heard birds chirping. He looked up. He saw a bird's nest.

"Watch, don't bother the baby birds," said Benny. "Come here. You need a bath."

But Watch wouldn't come.

Benny got some dog biscuits. "Watch," he yelled. "Do you want some biscuits?"

Watch's ears perked up. He ran over to Benny.

   Benny gave Watch three
biscuits. Then Benny held onto
him and gave him a good bath,
with lots of soap and water. "Now
your fur is soft," said Benny. "You
smell good, too."

After breakfast, Benny put
the costume on Watch.
Watch was waiting at the door.
Benny let him outside.

Watch ran over to the tree again. He started barking. Benny looked up and saw a cat. It was right by the baby birds! The cat jumped into another tree and ran down the trunk.

Watch chased the cat through the yard and into the woods.

"Watch, come back!" yelled Benny. "Your costume will get dirty!"

Watch ran out of the woods. His paws were dirty. His hat was missing. And his coat was ripped.

"Watch, you ruined your costume!" cried Benny. "It's time for the parade! What are we going to do now?"

But Watch didn't care. He ran back over to the tree. The baby birds started chirping again.

"Watch," said Benny, "I think you saved those baby birds! You're a hero! Just like Superman! That gives me an idea."

Benny got a small yellow blanket, paper, and paint. He asked Grandfather to help him spell. He made a sign. It said "Superdog." Then he painted a big S on the blanket.

"You can be Superdog," said Benny. He tied the blanket around Watch's neck. "And here's your cape. Now, let's go to the parade."

There were lots of people and
pets at the parade. Benny saw
cats, rabbits, dogs, and birds.
He even saw someone with a bowl
of goldfish.

The parade began. On the corner, Benny saw his friends Beth and Michael. He smiled at them. They clapped and waved as he walked by.

Down the street were the
judges. Benny smiled at them,
too. Watch wagged his tail.

At the end of the parade, Benny saw his family. They were waving, clapping, and cheering.

A judge came over to Benny. "Here's a ribbon for a very fun costume," she said. "Your dog is the perfect little superhero."

"Wow. My first pet parade," said Benny, "and we won a prize! You really *are* super, Watch."

"Woof!" barked Watch.

1309